The House of One Hundred Faces
and Other Spooky Poems & Short Stories

The House of One Hundred Faces

and Other Spooky Poems & Short Stories

W. M. Ashley

Edited by Bird and Bear.

eBook ISBN: 979-8-9919891-3-8
Paperback ISBN: 979-8-9919891-4-5

Any references to historical events, real people, or places are used fictitiously. Names, character, and places are products of the author's imagination.

Note of Content Warnings/Possible Triggers: moderate violence, references to capital punishment/child abuse (in "Confessions of Meadowhurst Asylum"), poems that contain reflections on madness and mental health, little to no romance, no swearing/profanity.

Front and back over image: stock photo from Pixabay.com.
Embellishments from Pixabay.com.
Clip art from Canva.com.
Cover design formatted in Canva.com.

First printing, 2025.

www.wmashleyauthor.com

DEDICATION

For my cousin Chelsey, a true storyteller. Thanks for telling me those "true" (a.k.a. the Brothers Grimm) versions of fairytales.

&

For my great-aunt Sandi, who loves all things Halloween.

STORY SYNOPSES

A TRUTH UNVEILED - An uninvited guest arrives to the wedding of a young bride and groom...but only the bride can see her.

LOYALTY: A TUDOR TALE - Imprisoned by her own sister Queen Mary in the dreaded Tower of London, Young Princess Elizabeth has a ghostly encounter in the very place where her own mother was brutally executed.

THE WITCH OF WILLOW WOOD - Hazed into joining an elite girl's club, a young woman finds herself trapped in the forest that homes a legendary witch.

CONFESSIONS FROM MEADOWHURST ASYLUM - Tales of abuse under mysterious circumstances are confessed through the eyes of various employees from a Native American reformatory.

THE DIARY I, THE GOVERNESS & THE GRAVEYARD, and THE DIARY II - Two tales 200 years apart are weaved together as a girl tries to make sense of the eerie nature of her new governess and a young woman finds a mysterious diary in a mausoleum.

THE SIRENS OF WHITBY - In the infamous seaside village that inspired Bram Stoker's *Dracula*, a young girl and her friend experience a deadly encounter.

THE MOURNER - A funeral director learns the monstrous history of a mysterious mourner who repeatedly attends wakes at his funeral home.

CONTENTS

ACKNOWLEDGMENTS

The short story "The Sirens of Whitby" was originally published in *Above, Below, and Beyond the Sea* (2024).

The short story "The Governess and the Graveyard" was originally published online by White Cat Publications, a Fireheart Company (2023).

The short story "The Witch of Willow Wood" was originally published in *Women of the Woods* (2020).

Thank you to my editor at Bird and Bear for all her hard work in editing my manuscript. I also want to express appreciation to my ARC readers for being willing to review my work.

Thank you also to my family and friends who have always supported my writing endeavors.

I want to acknowledge all my English teachers over the years who instructed me in the ways of crafting stories and weaving the English language into art.

And lastly, thank you to the readers who are currently taking a chance on my collection. I hope you enjoy!

The House of One Hundred Faces

The House of One Hundred Faces
gave me reason to pause,
while mystery dwelled in spaces
trapped in their imminent claws.

The first face I saw was kind;
she answered the door to my knock.
She bid me enter to find
those living behind the lock.

Though my heart thumped in rapid beat,
curiosity came, commanding my feet.

Paintings that hung on aging walls
held each face and eerie stare.
All ages; thin, fat, short, and tall;
eyes watched with pretentious care.

But surprise soon turned to dread.
When on the cliff of stairs, I stood,
an unseen hand pushed my head
and down the flight my body flew.

Here I wait for you to come…
now face one hundred and one.

2

Reflections on a Specter

Whispers from a faceless and timeworn past
Disturb me as I sit in solitude.
Here I thought that the loneliness would last,
But from seclusion called a multitude

Of souls unseen, yet somehow known to me
From lasting songs and cracked, callous pages;
From churchyard gravestones, the sightless can see
The bridge to earth from all the past ages.

One of them appears, a soul once thought dead;
A specter of shadow, devoid of blood,
Ethereal light from her feet and head;
Here she seeks refuge from Death's cruel flood.

The call soon ends at the church bell's last ring;
I'm again left alone, with Death's cold sting.

A TRUTH UNVEILED

I regard myself in the mirror, the sequins on my ivory wedding gown glistening under the crystal chandelier that hangs delicately from the ceiling. The Juliet cap veil on my head shimmers under its ambiance. The veil is my favorite part. Mother thinks it far too modern, suggesting I dress myself in something more traditional for a wedding in the year 1920. But this is the style now; everyone says so.

The hotel lobby, bursting with wedding guests, has transformed into a fairy palace. Flames from petite candles twinkle above me as I saunter through the garland-draped entryway, snowy voile adorning its arch. Many of the women in my party, sequined headbands glistening, also embrace the new flapper style that *Trendy Girl* magazine has declared as the popular look for "bright young things." *Told you so, Mother.*

Then I see him. The millionaire who asked for my hand, Alexander Beaumont Recine III, is dapperly dressed in a sleek tuxedo, his dark hair slicked back to show his dramatically handsome features.

Except someone else lingers behind him. The woman is draped in a veil of her own that has yellowed grotesquely. The thick shroud doesn't permit her face to be seen. Her matching dress—risen high to her neckline, sleeves puffed at the hems—makes me think she stepped out of a turn-of-the-century photograph.

No one from my audience appears to acknowledge this woman's presence. Alexander reaches out for my hands, welcoming me to the front of the platform, where the preacher stands. He gingerly puts my arm through his as we walk. The veiled woman follows us.

"Who is she?" I whisper to my fiancé, sparing a glance behind us.

"Who?" he inquires, checking over his shoulder.

"The woman in the veil," I answer, wondering if he is jesting.

"You're the only one in a veil, my darling," he counters. "Who else would be wearing one at a wedding?"

Alarmed, I lift the sheer fabric from my eyes to get a better look at the woman, but as my veil vanishes from my view, so does she.

A few gasps from the crowd follow and I wonder if it's from my shared shock at the disappearance of the specter or the fact I lifted my veil prematurely.

"*What* are you doing?" Alexander drops my arm and promptly pulls my veil back over my eyes. "That's *my* job, remember?"

He continues his stride to the preacher, but I do not follow. For as the white harbinger of doom is draped once more over my eyes, the woman immediately reappears.

As I contemplate whether it is my own veil causing me to hallucinate these strange visions, the act of breathing becomes a struggle, as if my breath is reluctant to escape my mouth.

Whispers from the crowd herald my swift exit as I dash back down the aisle and into the nearest restroom. I tear off my veil and splash water on my face to erase the image of the phantom in the wedding gown.

Who is she? Why can I only see her through the fabric of my

veil and not with my naked eye?

Alexander shortly joins me in the restroom, a look of astonishment outlining his handsome features. "What is the matter with you!"

I bury my fear and reveil my face. As I assumed would happen, the woman in the aged veil reappears by his side. "I should have said *I don't* instead of *I do*," a voice growls from beneath the discolored veil.

I turn to Alexander. "Were you married before?"

His shock intensifies. "*What?*" He must sense I am *dead* serious because he soon retracts. "Y-Yes," he stammers. "She died, but it was an accident. She was an alcoholic, and one night she drank so much it stopped her heart."

"He lies!" the bride exclaims.

I swallow the lump of fear that has been bulging in my throat and try to make sense of the situation. But I cannot. My selfish desire for this truth to be false causes me to remove my veil once more and erase the accusing spirit from my presence a final time.

I can feel my eyes redden as I gaze into my fiancé's own, and I whisper a question I'm dreading the answer to.

"Are you telling me the truth?"

"Of course," he says.

I believe him. It's my last mistake.

Before too long, I once again join Alexander down the matrimonial aisle, but this time, I am invisible to him. I am invisible to all. Another woman walks down the aisle towards us, her own white veil shielding her eyes from the scene. But I know she sees me.

8

Unmarked Grave

Just another blade of grass, I fold
beneath the soles of sightless shoes
that see no sinking flesh,
—nor dry or ivory bone—
just footprint casts on earthy marsh.

Like a victim of execution, I bow
while secrets on wagging tongues
burn my hollow ears and
encroaching feet are deaf
to my cry from beneath.

A patron's eye won't waste a tear
to find my missing name,
but bumps appear upon their
unwary skin all the same.

While unseen, I wait for them
to find my shell beneath
stifling soil until the day
comes when I am found.

The Executioner

I am Faceless
But the face of fate is etched into my façade

I am Nameless
But your names have branded my soul

I am Guiltless
But rebukes from my ghosts plague me

Forgiveness I do not deserve
But you willingly grant it as I field my office

12

LOYALTY: A TUDOR TALE

March 18, 1554

The last twenty-one years of my life spill over me, scattering my crimson hair in its wake. Mistress Blanche grasps my hand tightly as the tiny boat carrying me down the Thames shifts amidst the fog-laden current.

"Be strong, milady," I hear her plead. "God has not forsaken thee."

But her voice is a distant echo that disturbs my memories. Some of them seem so vivid: my unconquerable governess, Kat Ashley, teaching me French at my childhood home at Hatfield; the holly branch that my stepmother, Anne of Cleves, always wore in her hair at palace Christmas banquets; my stepmother, Katherine Howard, dancing while one of her ladies played the lute; and my stepmother, Catherine Parr's, soft voice as she read the words of Tyndale's Bible next to the warm hearth.

I hold these memories with me as the melancholic rhythm of the waves splashes against the small boat.

In the moments remaining before I reach my inevitable

destination at the godless Tower, I mercilessly try to sift through my past for the one person who I can not so vividly remember. The only memory I have of her is this: Raven-black hair curtains her pale face, her eyes glazed over from the tears that she struggles to keep from falling. She could be very beautiful, if only her countenance did not warrant such sadness.

This is the only image I could ever conjure of the woman who gave me life. Once a queen, she now remains gone forever, and I will no doubt be reunited with her sooner than I had ever wished upon my arrival at this wretched place.

The March wind catches in my throat as I set eyes upon the dark gate through which members of my own family had met their bloody end. And almost immediately, another figure resurfaces from my memory—one who I hoped would remain hidden in the deepest part of it. I can almost feel his thick, jewel-encrusted fingers grasp my hand and raise me from the curtsy I so habitually bowed into during every meeting. Although he may not have known it when he was alive, I could never find it in my heart to call him *Father*. It felt far too dangerous. Was it not he who had first labeled me a bastard in my childhood?

Just as I vowed to never reveal my fear to him, I must now refrain from showing any trace of anxiety at the expense of the new queen…the one too dangerous for me to call *Sister*. For it was she who sent me here.

All too soon, the boat halts at the stony steps of the fortress that welcomes all traitors into its entrapment—traitors who spend their last days entombed before their torture, confession, and eventual execution. I am now among the company of their ghosts and I, like so many of them before me, am innocent.

The boatman snatches the thick flaxen rope from its place at the bottom of the boat and thrusts it onto the platform near the steps. As he struggles to tie it off, my gaze drifts behind him and I catch a glimpse of the grisly severed heads of four of those alleged traitors—three of whom I do not even recognize— inhumanly mounted on pikes protruding out of the black water. My insides churn as they disappear behind the heavy clink of the portcullis. But the pain-stricken faces remain etched in my memory. *Be strong, Elizabeth*, I repeat in my mind. *God has not forsaken thee.*

The boatman's booming voice startles me out of my thoughts as he gruffly orders, "Out of the boat!"

The encouraging voice from my mind erupts out of my mouth before I give myself permission to utter the words. "Most certainly not!"

Thick drops of rain begin to pound the stone fortress and all I do is stay where I am in the swaying boat, pitilessly glaring at the man.

"If ye do not move, then I will move ye m'self…spoiled little—!"

"Lady Elizabeth!" comes another man's voice from up the steps.

I turn my head from the snarl of the boatman to an older gentleman's relaxed face, his white beard dripping from the sudden torrent. "I can attest that your quarters are far drier than the state of things out here."

I clutch the fabric of my bronze gown from each side and stiffly step from the boat onto the bottom stone stair that leads up to the fortress. "I will not move from this spot! Not for the fate we all know will eventually be thrust upon me!"

"That does it!" the boatman bellows. "She's your problem now, John!" He strips the rope from off the platform's peg, shouts an order to open the gate, and follows the current back out the way we came.

Seeing my last hope of escape drift away, I let my feeble legs give out from under me. The rest of my body slumps onto the top step of the pier. I position myself away from the bearded gentleman and wrap my arms around my knees.

"I beg of you, milady, please do not let yourself catch your death out here."

I defiantly straighten my back to him. "Save the executioner the ax, says I!"

He must understand my intention, because the next sounds I hear are his sloshing footsteps retreating away from me. I raise my head a little higher. *Maybe they will let me have my way after all.*

But I find my hope is in vain as the footsteps return, though a little lighter this time. "Elizabeth?"

I would have recognized that angelic voice anywhere, even in such an accursed place as this.

"…Kat?" My legs somehow regain their strength and I embrace my childhood governess.

Her eyes beam through a rain-soaked face as she throws a black cloak around my trembling frame. "Sir John Brydges is a good man. He will take care of you, I promise."

As much as I desire to argue, I believe her. At the peril of my own life, I must.

After the three of us enter through the doorway of what the warders call "Bell Tower," we ascend the stony steps to where my new quarters are located.

"Sir John?" I apprehensively address the white-bearded gentleman. "…Any word from the queen?"

Sir John removes his blue velvet cap and tries to slap what is left of the rain off of it. "And what word is Her Grace expecting?"

"I wrote to her two weeks ago, proclaiming my innocence. Surely, she cannot condemn me without proof."

"Milady." He lowers his voice. "I have been to the dungeon and questioned Sir Thomas Wyatt myself, and believe me when I say that he steadfastly claims that responsibility for the rebellion against your sister, the queen, does *not* rest with you."

He halts at the top of the stairs. "I suggest you pray that he *remains* true to that claim."

I rest my hand on the dank wall to steady my footing. "God bless his honesty. For I am truly innocent against any treachery to the queen."

Suddenly feeling uncomfortable asking questions about a condemned man who is residing within the same walls as I am, I change the subject. "Word reached my ears of the kindness you showed my cousin Lady Jane before she met her—" I cringe as an image of the axe falling upon my poor cousin's neck flashes into my mind, "—*unfortunate* end."

His eyes shift downwards. "She made it easy for me to do so. A complaint never escaped her lips, despite the frightening prospect of what was to become of her."

Sir John ushers me into the room where my two ladies are

waiting for me. Faint light streams in from a high window off to my left and two heavily armed yeomen guard both sides of the doorway.

"Your quarters, Lady Elizabeth."

Turning to dismiss him, I steal a glance over his shoulder and spot one of the much-rumored messages from a former prisoner etched into the wall. The message reads:

The Bell Tower showed me such sight
That in my head sticks day and night.
-   TW, 1536

Sir John notices my reading it. "That was written by Sir Thomas Wyatt, father of the Thomas Wyatt now in the dungeon."

I catch one of my ladies, Lettice, whisper to Lady Blanche, "He was here when her mother was imprisoned…"

My insides begin to boil again at the thought that this man who had left his mark had witnessed my own mother's execution. Perhaps his ghost will witness mine as well. I force myself to swallow down the fear rising in my throat.

"I trust…" I sputter to Sir John as he turns to leave, "that you will show the same kindness to England's princess that you have given to the Lady Jane."

April 10, 1554

Over the next few weeks, the blessing of continuing my studies with Kat becomes short-lived as I hear news that Sir Henry Bedingfield, one of the Tower's new constables, has bribed my guards to keep my governess away from me. Why, I cannot say. This snubs any last hope I have of regaining the lost months of my life. I even catch a glimpse of him trying to offer money to Kat himself.

I believe her when she visits me for the last time in the courtyard and protests the acceptance of any bribery at Henry's hands. I encourage her to leave for her own safety. Now my only human contacts are my ladies and Sir John.

A dreariness looms over me as I walk the long stretch of the hill leading up to Tower Green. I feel the souls of those pitiful victims of the Tower's torture on their way to the scaffold where the executioner's block rests. Whether their crime was against the Crown or in defiance of it, I cannot know, only that they all now unite in death.

I stop at the top of the hill, just a few paces from the wooden scaffold. A pool of deep scarlet stains the wood underneath the very block that now drowns my thoughts. I cringe at the thought of the last person who made the stain more vibrant—the rebel whose father left the message in my own chamber—and shudder at who the next prisoner to spill their blood might be.

"Rather foreboding, is it not?" comes a woman's voice from behind me.

I spin around, nearly falling over. "Who addresses me?"

The woman takes a few steps closer but keeps her distance. Her face is thin and fair, and her black eyes stare at me beneath lowered lashes, almost daring me to look. Her hair is concealed beneath the hood of an emerald cloak.

"I am a fellow prisoner like yourself."

I take one step backward. "Judging by the fine fabric of your cloak, are you nobility?"

Something near to a smile crosses her lips. "Once."

"Are you the wife of one of the warders?"

She remains silent.

I bite my lip, suddenly uncomfortable. "Do you know who *I* am?"

"Rumor reached me that Lady Elizabeth herself is gracing the Tower. That hair," she points to my fully exposed locks, "suggests that of a Tudor."

I take a strand of the red hair that has both beautified and haunted me since birth and sift it through my fingers. "Well, has rumor yet reached you that whether I am still a Tudor is in dispute?"

"Ah yes. Mary." At this moment, I am not sure if this woman is a traitor or a supporter of the Crown, but she must be imprisoned for a reason.

As if reading my mind, she continues. "Mary and I knew each

other through different circumstances. Ones I hoped would garner trust, but alas, that hope was dashed by the same coldness that has now consumed her heart."

I bury my face in my hands, trying desperately to restrain the tears that I have tried to keep at bay until now. "Then what am I to do? My mother was killed by my own *father!*" The word nearly chokes me. "My brother perished before his time, and now my own *sister—!*"

"Is dying," she cut in.

I lift my head from the shield of my hands and the woman's coal-like eyes meet mine.

"You too are the daughter of a king and can use this to your advantage. Hold on until her death, and then seize her power."

"Watch your tongue, my good lady!" I snap. "Talk like that will cost us both our heads! Besides," I add, dropping an octave, "to me, the reality of ever becoming queen will not mean *power*. I will instead gain something I desire above all else."

"And what is that?" she inquires.

"My freedom," I breathe.

She lets out an untimely giggle. "Wait until you are married. You will find that word will yield a far different connotation."

Hesitantly, I debate whether or not I should reveal the secret I had only ever entrusted to myself to keep. "I will never marry."

The woman reaches out her hand and relaxes it lightly upon my shoulder. "If I can hope to put any fears of yours to rest, know that you are safer in this prison than you realize."

For a moment, I consider shrinking away from her comforting gesture, perhaps reprimand her for it, but the familiarity I sense with this woman cannot be shaken. She is certainly someone who I have met before.

"Safe?"

"Even here you have friends in high places. Men have died and will die to protect you. I implore you not to doubt the loyalty of Sir John."

"I doubt the loyalty of everyone." I stiffly lift her hand from my shoulder, ushering her to recoil from my presence. "Especially those who refuse to tell me who they are."

With a subtle smile, the woman in the emerald cloak reveals

only what I have known all along: She knows something I do not. "One thing you have never need to doubt—I will always remain loyal to *you*."

She gives my hand a brief squeeze and then retreats to where I first encountered her at the top of the hill. Once there, she removes her hood.

I squint as the dark curtain of her hair rises with the same breeze that lifts my own crimson locks. It cannot be. Alarmed, I shift my gaze around the rest of the courtyard, hoping that someone else is also bearing witness to the presence of this person. Finding myself alone, I return my gaze to her.

Only the scaffold remains. No woman. No emerald cloak. No voice I before believed only existed in the memory of my childhood.

"…Milady?" A new voice calls out a few paces from behind me and I let out a shriek.

My sudden outburst startles poor Sir John, to whom the voice belongs. He holds a rolled-up piece of parchment in his clenched hand. "Why are you wandering the courtyard unaccompanied? Do you know how dangerous it is for you to be wandering the premises alone?"

"But I—" Surprised at the urgency of his tone, I try to explain myself but then stop, realizing the last thing my supporters need is to think their princess is seeing ghosts. I clear my throat. "I saw the grounds were vacant. What harm could come from taking a momentary stroll?"

Sir John grabs my arm without warning and leads me back down Tower Green towards Bell Tower. "No more risks! I am placing you inside your quarters where I can keep a better eye on you."

"What risks?" I sputter. His grip becomes tighter as we enter the stairwell leading up to my quarters. Surely this was not appropriate behavior for one of my "friends in high places" to exhibit.

"For your own protection," he answers, "I will remain mute to that inquiry."

The door flies open, and I stumble into my quarters where my ladies are gathered in the middle of the room. At the sight of me, they spring up from their huddled positions and throw their arms around my shaken frame. Judging by their pale expressions, something equally frightening must have happened to *them*.

"Thank heaven you are safe!" Lettice is trembling. She clutches my hands tightly and leads me to the back of the room with Blanche, away from the ears of the guards.

I am confused by their behavior. "After treatment like that, how safe can I possibly be?"

"Sir John is the one who just saved your life from that evil Sir Henry Bedingfield!" Blanche says with a moan.

Dread fills me. "What?"

"We were listening to Sir John talk to one of the other warders in the hallway, just before we got locked in here ourselves. Bedingfield tried to issue a warrant for your execution!"

The room begins to spin as my legs buckle. Both of my ladies catch hold of my arms to steady me. "Execution...?"

"But Sir John intercepted it before it could leave the Tower," Lettice continues, her voice quivering from the tears that now fill her eyes. "He saw the warrant in no way bore the queen's signature and seal, so it could not be used against you. He is looking for Bedingfield now to question him."

"She told me I could trust Sir John," I mutter as quietly as possible.

"Who?" Blanche asks, lowering her own volume as a tear escapes her cheek.

I peer at her and Lettice through the glossy film that now fills my own eyes. "My mother."

22

Salem

Crow covens cackle
At the tourists that trespass
On Poe's poetry,
And Hawthorne's havens,
Who authors antiquity
—Nineteen somber souls—
Autumn leaves crackle
Under stories of tour guides
—Heralds of the haunt—
While the scent of fire
And herbs steal the air and I'm
Reminded of fear

24

Musings of a "Witch"

I watch the road bow
up to my cottage abode.
Will a visitor

Grant me their presence?
Or will iron cage their hearts
as it often hath?

Tongues lashing out lies
like they did to my sisters
in Salem before?

Unyielding, I go
back to the thickening brew
and laugh to myself.

They'd think it evil,
but healing herbs never are.
…This should do the trick!

26

THE WITCH OF WILLOW WOOD

The time for accusation had passed, and it was now the moment when the truth had to be revealed. Mary wondered what the implications would bring, or if telling the townspeople what had truly happened in the marshes of the wood would eliminate the power the witch held over this town once and for all.

Three Days Before

Strange happenings always seemed to occur either near or inside the whispering swamplands of Willow Wood, and the ladies of the Bellham Society knew that. Many people would dare to think that these women used such tales to their advantage— even to go as far as *threatening* girls to join their club. Still, the prestigious reputation of the Society prevented people from murmuring these suspicions too loudly. The town was rather small, after all.

"Some say it would be an honor to join," Karina said to Mary one day, their parasols in hand.

"Perhaps," Mary muttered, warily. "Did they tell you what needed to be done on *your* part?"

"They want me to meet them tonight at midnight at the edge of Willow Wood for some sort of initiation."

Mary gripped her parasol handle tighter. *Initiation.* She had heard rumors about this word that had become taboo, even in her own household. Her mother had once spoken briefly about her own sister's initiation into the Bellham Society, not long after it was founded. Mary never knew her aunt, just that she had gone missing when she was Mary's age…and hadn't been seen since.

Mary had asked her mother about her aunt. Just the one time.

"What happened the night Aunt Celia went missing?" she asked after dinner one night.

Her mother would have kept her mouth shut in fear of frightening her own daughter, but after the Bellham Society sought to *recruit* Mary, she felt it was time to relate the story—for her daughter's safety.

"*She* took her," she answered while looking out at the cursed woods, so quietly that Mary wondered if it was an answer or a question.

"Who?" Mary inquired further, inching her body closer to the edge of her chair.

"The witch."

Mary gulped. "She's real?"

Her mother turned to her, something like panic peering out of her eyes. "Who else could it have been?"

For a moment, Mary thought her mother looked as young as she—uncertain, unknowing, and scared.

"After it happened," her mother continued, "the other members of the Society were very shaken up. They told me it was supposed to be a test. If she could survive the whole night in the swamp—not ten yards from the witch's cottage—then she would be accepted into the Society. But when they returned to the woods to retrieve her in the morning, she was nowhere to be found."

Mary could feel her teeth begin to rattle against one another. "W-what do you mean? What happened to her?"

Mary's mother placed a cold hand on her daughter's own clammy fingers. "The witch took her for her own."

Karina arrived at the edge of the forest almost three minutes late. What would they think of her tardiness?

"Is that you, Karina dear?" came a voice from behind her, farther into the woodland.

Karina turned to face Isabella Creed, the young blonde leader of the Society. The lantern she held illuminated her spotless white gloves and the signature pink ribbon tied at her waist. Four other girls flanked her, wearing the same white gloves and styling their own hair after Isabella's classically elegant bun.

"Yes." Karina swallowed, knowing it was too late to turn back now.

"Follow us," Isabella ordered in a sugary tone. Two of the girls from the group followed behind Karina as the other three led them farther into the unforgiving swampland. Karina peered over her shoulder at them suspiciously. What would they do if she tried to flee?

Casting out of her imagination the sudden fearful thoughts of white-gloved ladies chasing after her with battle-axes, she tried to keep her head in the present time. Where they were going had to be far worse.

The sound of six pairs of sloshing boots against the moist forest floor echoed throughout the looming willow trees that looked far more ghostly against the onyx backdrop of night. If they ventured any farther, they would be within the borders of the witch's domain.

"Stop," Isabella ordered the party, and the two girls who followed Karina each flanked her right and left side. "Hold her," she told them.

Each girl grabbed one of Karina's arms and held tightly. Karina struggled at first, but then realized it was no use. They said it was an initiation, so they would not *kill* her…right?

"Tonight, we welcome a new pledge into our prestigious

Society," Isabella said, facing Karina, a twisted smirk on her red lips. "As you know, we are looking for a sixth member to make our sisterhood complete. Complete your task tonight, and you are guaranteed membership."

"T-task?" Karina sputtered, failing to hide her fear.

"About six yards away lies the dwelling of the Witch of Willow Wood. The woman who has dwelt in these woods for over a hundred years. The one who casts spells on any who disturb her solitude and who may or may not make you into a pie for her next meal."

The other girls giggled in response, and Karina could have sworn she caught a glint of red in Isabella's eyes as her smirk intensified.

She then felt any courage that was left leave her. She struggled against her captors' grips, but they were too strong, too determined to intensify her terror.

"Restrain her!" Isabella barked at the remaining two girls, who retrieved a thick piece of rope that had been hidden behind the nearest willow tree. The two girls who held Karina in their grip pushed her body against the tree's trunk, allowing the others to wind the rope around her. Only when she was tethered tightly to the tree did they loosen their grips.

Karina readied her voice to scream, but her fear of *who* might hear her cries prevented her from doing so.

"Since you are not going to camp out here of your own volition, we will just have to let the forest decide your fate," Isabella sneered, inching towards her until they were at eye level. "And keep it down. You wouldn't want to be the witch's breakfast, would you?"

The others continued to giggle after Isabella as they, and sadly, the only source of light in the wood, followed her out of the hellish swamp.

For a bog, it was eerily quiet. No music from a cricket nor croak from a frog sounded. Even they must have sensed the horrific things the witch was capable of.

Karina tried to keep her breathing steady, but paranoia began to crowd her mind. Which way was the witch's cottage? Had she heard any of the girls' voices from her dwelling? Did the witch enjoy eating girls her size? How would Karina get out of here? Which way was home? Was that a footstep behind her or just a frog splashing in the mulch?

Dizziness soon overtook her. *Maybe it is better if I just pass out*, she decided. But before she could follow through with her plan, a *psst* sounded in her ear.

Her voice grew hoarse as she asked "Who is there?" in a quivering tone.

"Who do you think, the Witch of Willow Wood?" came the voice she knew belonged to her friend Mary.

Relief overtook Karina and then disappointment. "What are you doing here?"

"Saving you from your own destruction, of course."

Karina heard the back-and-forth motion of a small sharp object against twine, followed by the rope that bound her against the tree loosening. "No! If you free me, then I will never be one of them."

Mary groaned in the darkness. "You are not still considering *becoming* one of those witches, are you?"

Karina remained silent in protest. She could not help it. It was the biggest paradox she had ever encountered. She knew what she was doing degraded her self-respect in almost every way. Still, there was something about the flawlessly beautiful Isabella and the confident loyalty of her cronies that drew her in. It was something she did not know how to explain to Mary, or even to herself.

"Come on," Mary urged Karina as the last bit of rope fell to the damp forest floor.

"How did you find me?" Karina asked as the two of them sloshed farther through the marsh, disorientation setting in for the both of them.

"I followed Isabella's lantern that led you here. Unfortunately, after she left, I didn't have the faintest idea where she went."

Karina squinted against the darkness, her panic returning. "Then we are stuck here. What if the witch finds us?"

Mary began to sense her friend's apprehension, and her mother's words from long ago returned to her in a rush of anxiety all her own. "Come, I think they may have gone this way."

She took her friend's hand and headed for a gap between two large willow trees. For what seemed like an eternity, they weaved through trees, bushes, and other unrecognizably dense objects in the woodland, all different shades of black against the night.

They both began to think they would never escape, until suddenly they noticed a small gleam of green light ahead of them.

"Look," Karina whispered. "The fireflies have come to light our way. We must finally be out of the witch's domain."

Mary breathed in the thick air of the swamp, relieved. But as they approached the light, she realized their respite was short-lived. The closer they strode towards the light, the larger it grew, until it completely blocked their path. But it did not stop growing. Both girls were afraid to touch it. There was something about it that seemed to encompass them, as if daring them to escape.

Mary and Karina were on the verge of screaming for release, when a figure approached them through the static of the lime-green mist. The haggard being wore a long brown tunic, her black hair gathered in clumps down her back. Her dark eyes held an expressionless stare and her face twisted into a grin. The last sound that emanated from Mary and Karina were their unrestrained screams before the three of them disappeared into the darkness.

Mary awoke to the snores of Karina, who was sleeping not too far from where her own body lay on a dirt-covered floor. Outside, a faint light beamed down through a crack in between two wooden shutters. Before she could give her whereabouts further thought, she heard the steps of an unknown being on the other side of the wood door in front of her. Then she remembered that night, the mist, and the witch.

"Karina!" she shouted, seizing her friend's shoulder. "Wake up! Now!"

It did not take long for Karina to arrive at her senses. Mary could see the same panic that she felt emanating from her friend as the footsteps suddenly halted outside the door. Then, slowly, the wooden door creaked open, showing a glimpse of the face that had haunted the town's legends for so many years. But it did not look old—not much older than Mary's mother. Just dirty. And pale. Like she had not seen the sun for many seasons.

"H-hello?" was all Mary could say.

The witch creaked open the rest of the door. She held a tray of potions…no wait…was it *food?* Perhaps she wanted to fatten them up before she feasted on them for her main meal.

"Do you know who I am?" the woman asked, her voice surprisingly calm, and almost melodic.

Mary and Karina exchanged puzzled glances.

"Um, aren't you the Witch of Willow Wood?" Karina asked in a shaky voice.

The witch paused for a moment and then smiled. "Why don't you decide for yourselves?" she asked, setting down the plate of food.

Unexpectedly, she slowly removed the tangled black hair that crowned her head. Both girls gasped at the beautiful gold hair underneath. The witch then took off her mud-colored tunic, exposing an aged gray lace dress.

"A wig? A costume?" Karina scoffed. "Is this some kind of a joke?"

The woman sat down next to the girls on the floor. "Many years ago, I was found by the 'Witch of Willow Wood,' as this town calls her, and she provided a refuge for me from the real witches who haunt this town. Some of the descendants of whom I am sure you girls have already had the pleasure of meeting."

"The Bellham Society," Mary inferred.

The woman nodded.

Mary inched closer to the strange woman, realization flooding her consciousness. "*You* are my Aunt Celia."

34

Check-In

Have I gone mad? Yes,
they assure me. So, I sign
on the faded line.

Sanity (Variation on Jos Charles' "A Sonnet")

I wait in the wings
windows, doorways
seated in the bent
chair, or walking for
hours, naming the cracks
in the floor. When misery
came and went in 1999, my hope
dwindled like time in the halls. But the
year still came and went, I, cautiously, wait
ed for something to happen. He'd look at me tragical like
one staring at a sinking ship upon the horizon.
He'd refer me inevitably to another, another more
but the writing's on the wall; I didn't like
how he stared at the floor.

36

House of A Hundred Faces II

Night seeks to swallow the moon
As my face pales at the sight
Of the first face I see
Beyond the dimming light

As the threshold I cross,
More come into view
—Faces unknown to me—
But they won't remain new

Pale faces and paler coats
Fill my panicked sight
My bones this fear will chill
With every passing night

The noise of silence
Wakes my restless sleep
While peace claws at the doors
And through the walls it creeps

No one tells, yet eyes still find me
The monster in my mind
Longing for release
From the pale coats of humankind

Do they know my soul
Or the fear inside
Of the skull that holds
Where my monster hides?

Or can they try to make anew
The soul inside that seeks for truth?

38

CONFESSIONS FROM MEADOWHURST ASYLUM

Welcome to Old Meadowhurst Asylum Museum and Gift Shop, home of the mad, the creepy, and the weird," I mumbled, monotonously, just like I had for four summers prior. "How many are in your party?"

One of the teenagers in the group pushed his way to the front and leaned an arm on the counter. "So, which one are you? Mad, creepy, or weird?" he joked as his friends chuckled behind him. I narrowed my eyes slightly. Like I hadn't heard that one before.

"How many are in your party?" I repeated a little louder, careful to keep my face neutral. I glanced over at my phone, checking the time. Only one more hour left.

I tore the group's receipt from the printer and granted each annoying teenager access to the museum by stamping their hands with the insignia of Meadowhurst Asylum—a wrought iron gate with the letters M and A at its center.

"Think we'll see the ghost of one of these freaks?" one of the teens teased her neighbor, pointing to the wall of faces that lined the entryway.

Ghosts. Everyone who comes here comes with the notion that they will see the spirit of one of the asylum's many former residents. I cocked my head, looking at the photographs of these supposed "freaks." "Teary-Eyed Tina" from 1953 looked through her glossy eyes back at me, no doubt tired from the many nights she spent weeping in her cell. "Mark, the Masked Masochist" from 1910 glared at me through the homemade mask that he had fashioned to hide the burns on his face.

The air around me felt heavy as I continued to scan the wall. Patients aged five and older had walked these crumbling hallways, and whether people believed it, I knew the truth. While many other asylums may have housed authentic cuckoo clocks, Meadowhurst Asylum never had. This was the place where they put the people they were ashamed of. People who knew too much. People who could get them into trouble. Somehow, in the olden days, it seemed passing someone off as insane was easier than locking them away to keep them silent.

But we will never be silenced, she had told me that night. I was young and naïve, not much different from the teenagers who I just admitted, and I had thought these were truly disturbed individuals who had died without their mental faculties. Well, they may have died or left here insane…but I now knew that they didn't arrive that way.

Patient #173: "Mortimer"
Method: Lobotomy
15 March 1910

I would have winced, but once the sharp metal spike penetrated my skull, my face had already gone limp. Afterwards, I could not blink, but simply gazed ahead like a cadaver as Dr. Billingsworth spoke to his comrade.

"Did it work?" his redheaded, rat-faced intern remarked to him as his upturned nose filled my vision.

The doc, nearly blinding me with a small flashlight, addressed me. "Mortimer?" he inquired. I remained silent. "Yes, I think that did the trick. He won't be talking."

I guess they had a good reason to shut me up. I knew more than anyone else about the horrors of the Branthwaite Boarding School; I had been one of the ones who had committed them. They had done this so I would no longer remember. But I did. And I couldn't tell them.

"Does the paralysis last long?" Rat-Face asked the doc, wiping the sharp end of the pick clean with a damp cloth.

"Difficult to say," the doc answered. "But with this one, that may be something that could work to our advantage. I suggest hourly check-ins with him, just in case he regains more than just his motor functions."

"Understood, Doctor," Rat-Face answered, a gleam of something sinister in his eye.

Part of me hoped that I would never regain the use of my voice in case these two were intent on finishing me off. Because I knew as well as they that if my voice did return, I would shout from the rooftops of the atrocities committed at the Branthwaite Boarding School.

"Dr. Greer." Lord Branthwaite lifted his portly body from his cushioned chair and approached me, holding out his hand.

His eyes seemed kind enough, the wrinkles around them almost hiding them due to his wide grin. "We are very pleased to have you join us at this institution."

"Please, sir, call me Mortimer," I insisted, happy I could help him in his endeavor to civilize the local Native children that had dwelt in ignorance for far too long.

"Very well, Mortimer," Branthwaite agreed before ushering me to the seat opposite his ornate cherrywood desk. "We have much to discuss."

As I seated myself and placed my black leather gladstone bag under my chair, I couldn't help but notice the photographs hanging on the wall that stared back at me over Lord

Branthwaite's shoulder. In one, a row of gentlemanly-dressed Native American boys, about the age of thirteen or fourteen, stood together. Two nuns in their white habits stood on each side of them, smiling. I looked more intently at the group of young men and couldn't help but notice the dichotomy between how I had witnessed Native Americans look and the ones staring back at me. Each boy's formerly long black hair was cut short and each of their tattooed hands held a book or a bible. They were not smiling.

Branthwaite noticed my staring and took a gander at the photograph himself. "*That* is a good indicator of what you can expect from the outcomes we have made possible here. Civilizing the savages of our nation has proved tricky in the past, but we have finally found the right way to do it."

My interest was now piqued. "The *right* way?" I implored.

"Indeed," Branthwaite answered. "That is why I have brought you here."

A smile then tugged at his lips, and something all too ominous arose behind his eyes. "I trust that you will help us *whip* these heathens into shape?"

Branthwaite saw me wince. "The outcome soon turns into obedience. How else would they learn?"

Confusion flooded me. I knew all about capital punishment as a tool in classrooms, but to witness nuns and other church folk employed at this institution exhibit such behavior was certainly new to me. "So, is that why you requested my employment? To see to the injuries?"

Branthwaite guffawed, much to my surprise. "Of course not. You are here so when questions arise from outside parties about the goings-on in our institution, you can simply *say* that is why you are here."

Patient #156: "Sister Sarah"
Method: Ice Treatment
27 Jun 1903

Frozen. Knives seem to pierce my skin as they submerge my body beneath the ice. My feet can't help but flail against the porcelain bottom of the tub as my senses explode beneath the water's edge. Am I alive or dead? I cannot tell until my breathing recommences.

I think a scream escapes my throat, but all I hear is the pulsating thump of my own heart beating against my eardrums. No matter how many times a day they submerge me, the effect remains the same: near-death.

"What is your name?"

I hesitate but I worry they will submerge me again if I don't answer truthfully. "S-Sarah," I sputter, mouthfuls of icy water spilling out of me as I do.

"*Just* Sarah? What is your profession?"

I know what they want me to say. They want me to tell the truth. But I will not. I picture myself in the nun's habit and crucifix at my waist that all the nuns wore as we forced the Native children to recite the Lord's Prayer. I tremble at a recent memory of an eleven-year-old girl who refused to do so and instead sung the prayer of her people in her Navajo tongue. It was beautiful. But I could not let her or the others know that. *I* would be punished, or worse.

I remember taking the strap to her knuckles until she stopped singing. Tears filled my eyes at the thought. But I knew that she got off easy. There were far worse punishments that we were instructed to give to the children who would not comply. Punishments that I did not have the stomach to obey.

The man in the white jacket narrows his eyes at me, still waiting for me to respond. I fake a confused expression; it is my only defense. "I…I don't remember."

The two other orderlies holding my shivering arms look at him, awaiting his orders. I do as well. He relaxes his face and makes room for the orderlies to surround the tub once more.

"Again," he instructs, and I plunge once again into icy oblivion.

The new doctor stared down from Branthwaite's window at

me. Branthwaite was watching too. It seemed he was always watching.

I turned my back to the window. I wanted no more of this. But I couldn't just *leave*…they would make me disappear, just like they had so many other "teachers." Another thought entered my mind: What if I simply flee in the dead of night? That would surely give me a head start to alert the authorities, wouldn't it?

I kept these thoughts to myself as Sister Margaret and I corralled the rest of the students back inside for lessons. I couldn't trust her with my plan. I couldn't trust anyone.

Patient #289: "Arthur"
Method: Electroshock Therapy
3 August 1916

Another jolt sends fire through my brain all the way to the tips of my fingers. At this point, I feel like I can tell them everything I know, whether it is relevant to their questioning or not. For a moment, I cannot remember why I am here—or my name, for that matter—but I know that it must have been important to them. Why else are they subjecting me to this torture?

All this morning I had been questioned. First with questions pertaining to who my parents were, where I was born, and other personal details. But as my answers became less sure, the inquiries gradually changed to ones that pertained to more recent endeavors: *What did you do yesterday?* and *When did you last use the lavatory?*

After the last jolt of lightning finally leaves my body, I hear the all-too-familiar voice in my ear once more.

"Now," the man in the white coat addresses me calmly, "what exactly did you have for breakfast this morning?"

I had heard rumors about the terrors of the boarding school across town that sought to "civilize" the natives on our land. I had known about others across the country but was baffled to think that our town could harbor such derision. Surely, the institution here employed humane methods to educate the young, not the barbarous torture that was rumored to exist in the other Native American boarding schools. My assumptions proved to be wrong.

My source was a nun who had worked there as a teacher. She informed me of all kinds of atrocities the poor students suffered at the hands of those who sought to "civilize" them, and she was adamant that the truth should be published for all the country to see. My notes and recordings were still piled in the drawer of my desk. I didn't get to publish them. Yet.

Patient #363: "Lady Branthwaite"
Method: Isolation/Restraint
13 December 1927

Darkness. No matter how I try to adjust to it, it remains the same. Was that a voice or a distant echo? How long have I been here? I struggle against the invisible restraint that binds my arms to my torso. The room smells as stale as the office where my husband works.

I chuckle at the thought. Work. That was all my husband did, and I was proud of him. Educating the heathen children that overran our land was quite an honorable profession. It was the Lord's work, after all. Or that was what I had always thought. Not a day goes by when I do not think about my husband's idea of "the Lord's work." Images of frightened boys and girls as we chopped off their beautiful dark hair entered my mind. I once caught a boy no older than six chanting in his native tongue, but I refused to do anything about it. My husband caught me.

He kept a close eye on me after that; then, afraid he could not trust me, he sent me here. I have a feeling I will be the last.

Patient #124: "Jane Doe"
1 September 2022

"What is your name?" the strange girl in men's clothing asks me as I attempt to hide behind the rotting iron bars of the nearest cell.

"I have many names," I whisper.

"*Many?* Were you a schizophrenic?" she asks.

Puzzled, unfamiliar with the strange word, I shake my head.

"They call me Jane," I say.

"They?"

"The doctors. They gave me that name when I got here. But before that they called me Mary."

"Did you have a name before that?"

"My mother named me Snowbird."

The strange girl takes a step towards me, a somber look on her face. "Were you one of the students at Branthwaite Boarding School?"

I wince at the name. I had not heard it for quite some time, but hearing it now sends a sharp pang of fear to my heart. I noiselessly nod my head.

The girl kneels in front of me as if she is trying to coax a wounded animal out from under a bush. "What did they do to you?"

"What they did to all of us. Forced us to obey the rules and customs of the white man, or else we would be severely punished."

"Were you the first child to come to this asylum?"

I nod again. "I escaped to try to find the rest of my tribe. But *they* found me first. Once they discovered I was from the boarding school, they put me in here with the others."

"Others?"

"A journalist, the headmaster's wife, one of the teachers, and a doctor. They tried to keep us silent. But we will never be silenced."

Paranoia

Stomach roar
Brain pulse
Heart rupture
        at the feeblest sound

Curtain float
Silence beat
Steps tap
        the cold dead ground

Rush
Wait   and
Plead
        for escape

Freeze
Twitch and
Search
        for hands that won't come

Plunge
        into shame
        at the sound of your name

Sprint
        to the flame
        you ran from

The Door at the End of the Hall

Through the dark the light from it cuts
Behind   it   rusty   hinges   stay
…Is it open or is it shut?

Will   I   remain   in   this   guessing   rut?
Beyond   the   age   and   decay
Through the dark the light from it cuts

I   know   what   lays   inside   but
Will   my   mind   trust   today
That it will remain shut?

My   heart   drops   into   my   gut
Am   I   brave   enough   to   stay?
Through the dark the light from it cuts

Curiously   quickened   feet   jut
From   behind   the   cracked   ray
…Is it open or is it shut?

There   it   waits   until   time   rebuts
And   the   veil   of   ages   rues   the   day
Through the dark the light from it cuts
…Will it remain shut?

Musings of a Ghost

Asleep, yet awake
Invisibly I wander
Hoping to be seen

50

THE DIARY, PART I

"A *cemetery?*" my husband Tom incredulously inquires as we approach the gates of Père Lachaise. "We're spending a day in Paris to see a *cemetery?*"

Upon entering, the graveyard is so massive that actual street signs adorn the main cobblestoned drag of this *city* of the dead. Eventually, curiosity takes over as we meander off the beaten path and start our hunt for the famous graves of Oscar Wilde and Frédéric Chopin.

Camera in hand, I drink in the statues, tombstones, and decrepit family mausoleums sweltering in the Parisian noonday sunshine. Despite the light that illuminated the graves, a darkness seemed to loom over the gravestones. Attempting to ignore the intimidating stares of the statues gawking at us in the shadows, I try not to fall too far behind Tom. Some structures look brand new, while others look like they have stood since the dawn of time. Behind one of these crumbling edifices, a gray blur of movement catches my eye. Rationalizing that it is probably just another tourist, I ignore it and move on before I completely lose sight of Tom.

And then…there it is. A tall stone crypt surrounded by a black iron fence emerges before us. Some of the faded royal blue and jade stained-glass windows lay shattered, which makes it easier for the curious passersby to peer inside at the residual tombs. The inscription *Vivi Ex Mortuis* is etched above the domed doorway.

Hesitantly, I walk through the small open gate and peer through one of the broken windows into the strange edifice, but a strong feeling of fear soon takes hold, causing my feet to retreat backward.

"The Living Dead," Tom remarks as he flanks my shoulder, causing me to nearly jump right out of my skin. I stare at him in response.

"That's what *Vivi Ex Mortuis* means, Jenny," he expounds, noticing my puzzled expression.

And then something deep inside me shudders. "What person would want that engraved on their tomb?" I ask, my question directed more at the mausoleum than my husband.

"The Victorians were a weird bunch" is all he can come up with. He must be losing interest because he begins to walk past the strange structure and back onto the cobblestoned path. "Let's keep going. I want to see how weird Oscar Wilde's grave is."

"I'll catch up," I respond, wanting to explore this eerie building further.

"You'll get lost," he counters. "This place has to be at least a mile long."

"Just stay on the main path. I won't be long."

Tom shrugs his shoulders and starts back down the path at a slow pace. Then, after he turns the corner, a small breeze lifts the ends of my auburn hair.

I follow the direction of the breeze, which leads me towards one of the broken windows of the abandoned mausoleum. Apprehensive, yet curious, I peek inside. Nothing. No…there *is* something. I reach inside and pull it out. An old—*very* old—leather-bound book, no bigger than both of my hands combined, rests in my palms. Its brown exterior is matted with dust from an age undetermined.

The spot of gray I saw earlier moves once again, behind the broken window of the mausoleum, and this time, I catch what—

or *who*—it is. A young girl's face stares back at me. Her face is so caked with dust it gives her skin an ashen hue. She can't be more than ten years old. At first, I think it is a young tourist who got trapped inside after escaping her parents' watch. But then I see what she's wearing and reconsider. A deep gray dress covers her small figure, and a high collar conceals her throat. The fact that her ensemble is devoid of any color makes me think I am looking at an old photograph.

The phantom shifts her gaze from my eyes to the tiny book in my hand and she raises a dainty finger to point to it. I open the leather cover, careful not to damage any of the binding, and see a photograph of a young girl who matches the apparition before me.

I hear her whisper, *Read.*

I obey the voice and begin to read the writing on the first delicate page…

54

THE GOVERNESS AND THE GRAVEYARD

12 October 1846, 9:52 a.m.

Today Mother hired a new governess. Though she is younger than my former governess, Hilda, something about her feels old. She always dons upon her head a black bonnet trimmed in silky blue lace, and her face holds a pale, thin complexion.

But why did Hilda quit? She has been my governess ever since I was born, and then she flies from our home without so much as a "farewell"? Where had she gone?

Although I have yet to discover why Hilda quit, I find there is something strange about this new governess. In my history lesson today, when I asked her about King Louis XVI and Marie Antoinette's downfall, she commented, "If Antoinette had taken my advice, then she would have limited her spending habits," followed by, "...I mean to say, if someone would have told her that, then maybe she would have kept her head..."

13 October 1846, 12:40 a.m.

I have awakened from a nightmare. It is not one after which I can fall so easily back to sleep. And so, I write.

In my dream, a woman led me down a long, shadowy corridor. Her thin body, ashen face, and black bonnet trimmed in blue lace resembled that of my governess. I took her cold hand as she led me through an aging wooden door at the end of the hallway. It opened of its own accord.

The door creaked open to reveal a bare room, its walls painted onyx black. In the middle of the space, the only object that lay before us was a small coffin. To my horror, it was open. And empty.

I gasped as I realized its silk lining matched the blue lace of my governess's bonnet. "Get in," her haunting voice echoed.

I was soon back in the comfort of my own bed, though it was, at the moment, anything but comfortable. My pillow was soaked with the sweat of my trembling brow and my blanket had been flung from my bed in the night, leaving my twelve-year-old body shivering in the cold. Never had a nightmare shaken me so deeply. It felt so genuine, but it could not have been real…could it have?

16 October 1846, 5:00 p.m.

My governess and I were in a carriage accident today. Dare I say that I saw my governess die—or at least, she should have. Ever since that awful moment, thoughts of who—or what—my governess truly is have lingered in the recesses of my imagination.

We had just finished some errands she wished to complete before the weather got too torrential. How she knew what the weather would be like after the sunny morning we had experienced, I can scarcely imagine. The rain beat violently down on the dirt before us, making the ground so slick that the horse staggered, causing our carriage to tumble sideways into the muddy street. My governess was flung from the carriage shortly before the demise, her body trampled under the steed's heavy hooves. Then, a giant thump of the carriage wheel caused me to nearly fly from the vehicle as well.

Once the carriage had finally stilled, laying sideways in the sludge, I poked my head out of the left window to see my governess's mangled body behind the carriage. Struggling out of the vehicle, I approached the ghastly scene.

Her eyes lay wide open, her neck twisted against her blue-laced bonnet and her waist flattened against one of her arms. Hesitantly, I poked one of her white cheeks. It was dead to the touch.

Suddenly, I recoiled in horror as a gasp of air escaped my governess's mouth and her eyelashes fluttered. My heart nearly stopped at the sight of it. In a horrible, mangled thrashing of limbs, her body twisted back to its rightful frame, followed by a sickening cracking noise.

Panicked, I looked around for help and could see the carriage driver and a shopkeeper rushing towards us, the same shudder in their eyes.

"Y-you're all right, miss?" came the carriage driver's stuttering inquiry to my governess.

"Well of course I am all right!" she answered in her light tone, laughing off the whole incident like she had tripped on her skirt instead of suffering a crushing blow from a carriage wheel.

"Luckily I was thrown from the buggy before the horse could trample me," she lied. Then her eyes turned on me, as if daring me to tell the man what I had seen. "Are you alright, sweetie?"

"I do not know," I answered truthfully.

She did not speak of how she had survived this wretched death; she instead demanded that I do not relay to Mother and Father or anyone else what had occurred this day. But as I sit here scribbling, I know that I cannot remain quiet. And so, I put my pen to paper, hoping that by doing so, I may somehow erase this haunting incident from my memory.

20 October 1846, 5:36 p.m.

My governess fell down the stairs today. Before the occurrence, I was writing *I will not let my imagination run away with me* two hundred times in my notebook after I accidentally made the remark to my governess that she should have died in the carriage accident. Apparently, my tongue is a dangerous instrument against her. And here I was thinking that nothing could hurt this woman.

I was writing this line somewhere in the fifties when a heavy tumble against our wooden steps beckoned me to the hallway. By the time I got to the top of the stairwell, I saw my governess lying on the downstairs landing. The sight of her ankles twisted against her boots at that unnatural angle returned to me the gruesome details of what had happened four days before.

But I hesitated this time. Peeing over the ledge, I waited until I heard the same cracking of bones and flailing of limbs that had occurred after the carriage accident. After my governess snapped back to her full frame once again, I ducked out of sight before she could see my horrified gawking. She would not have been able to lie about her strange ability twice in one week.

22 October 1846, 8:42 p.m.

I have found myself becoming far more of a snoop as of late. I have also found myself becoming desperate to know exactly how or why this woman seems indestructible.

Today after my governess went home, I managed to steal a peek at her desk. All the books inside the top drawer seemed normal enough: *Advanced Mathematics, English for Beginners, Teaching Latin.* I then opened the bottom drawer to find one book that was not so normal.

Necromancy was all the title read. Is this how she disposed of my former governess— casting a spell on her so she would leave? And did she wish to teach me this forbidden art or use it against me in retribution for an incident I was not supposed to have witnessed?

Afraid of what nasty spell might come upon me if I were to even touch the book, I slammed the desk drawer shut, hoping that no traces of what I had seen remained.

29 October 1846, 2:15 p.m.

I find it curious that before Hilda left, she had lived and slept in my home, yet this governess refuses to do so. To gather more insight on this inconsistency, I spoke with my friend Mildred today, who said that her governess also lives in her home. Strange.

"Do you mean she has never stayed overnight?" she inquired.

"I do not believe so," I answered. Come to think of it, I had never seen her in our home past six o'clock. She never even stayed for dinner, but simply came for morning lessons, ran errands in the afternoon, and then left us before the sun went down.

Tomorrow after she leaves, I will follow her. Perhaps by doing so, I may not only discover where this Being lives, but it may also shed more light on her curious nature.

30 October 1846, 10:45 p.m.

Donning my black overcoat, bonnet, and rain boots, I followed my governess into the night. Strangely, she set out on foot. She must not have lived far. She crossed the street past the bakery and stopped at the gate to Père Lachaise Cemetery.

I gulped. I had never set foot in that graveyard before, but I had heard stories of the ghosts and demons within the graves that rested above the ground. What was she doing there after dusk?

My governess unlatched the chain that encased the rusty iron gate. The hinges squeaked as she entered the dark neighborhood of the dead. Mustering any resolve left within me, I followed.

In the darkness, I could just make out the gothic shapes of sorrowful statues standing guard at the entrances of old family crypts, decaying from time and neglect. But I did not linger on these shapes for long, for my governess was nearly out of sight; soon I would be doomed to roam among the dead until morning.

She turned down one of the cobblestoned conduits that led away from the main path. Down an alleyway of crypts at least six feet high she briskly walked, as if this place were her own neighborhood.

Amidst the black night, my senses heightened. Sounds of crackling leaves behind me led my gaze away from the path I was pursuing, only to leave me guessing which way my governess had headed. As I squinted against the dark, it was as if the statues of grief-stricken angels and crumbling gargoyles had grown five times larger and were set on blocking my escape. I struggled hard against the decision of whether I should let out a cry but thought better of it. I refused to take this venture again, so I could not let my governess find me following her.

Suddenly, I heard the subtle squeak of…the opening of a second gate? Yes. I shuffled over to where I heard the noise and saw the shadow of my governess again. She approached a large mausoleum that contained a single candle flickering in one of the stone-encased stained glass windows. Above the flickering light, the words *Vivi Ex Mortuis* glistened in the crimson glass.

A few moments after she had entered the strange crypt, my curiosity took over and I entered the structure. Inside the crypt, five relatively new mahogany coffins were positioned in a circle, each labelled with a date from this year. Hesitantly, I grabbed the candle set in the sill of the stained glass window and peered closer at one of the coffins until I could read the newly plated inscription. I nearly dropped the candle at the sight of it: *Hilda Franz, d. 1846.*

A gasp built in my throat, and I bit my gloved hand, fearing that the gasp would evolve into a scream. So, my new governess did get rid of Hilda.

But where was my new governess now? Pondering the possibility that she might have evaporated into the air, I felt a small sense of relief. But it was soon dashed by the echo of a sliding noise below my feet. Was there another floor below this landing?

Raising the candle higher, I saw against the far wall of the mausoleum were stone steps that led downward. *Down…* I gulped, and with a courage I did not know I still possessed, I descended the stairs.

Once at the bottom, I gagged against the smell of rotting flesh. My governess was nowhere to be seen, but rotting coffins, much older than the ones I saw aboveground, lined the walls. Dust caked the lids of each one and rusty brass handles hung from each side. Engraved under the stone slabs of each were no names, just dates. The oldest I saw still visible belonged to the year 1213. While the date suggested it was the oldest coffin in the crypt, the inch of dust that caked the other tombs' lids was strangely absent from this one. And there, on a rusty nail protruding out of the side of it, hung a familiar, blue-laced bonnet.

62

THE DIARY, PART II

I look up from the withering diary and am aware again of my present-day surroundings. The girl in gray is gone.

I inch closer to the now crumbling ruins of the haunting mausoleum. Poking my leg through the shattered window, I squeeze through the opening until I am standing inside the crypt. To my horror, five rotting wooden coffins are positioned in a now familiar circle. I hesitate as I approach the nearest one, what's left of the gold-plated inscription glistening in the afternoon sunlight as if daring me to read it. I squint at it and hold my breath as my mind formulates the only word I can make out beneath the rust: *Hilda.*

My hands automatically clutch the leather book, still present in my sweaty grasp, and I turn to face the back wall of the mausoleum where I already know a set of stairs reside. The sight of them flips my stomach. But before I can venture further down this rabbit hole of horror, I hear my name.

"Jenny!"

My musings over this strange building and its even stranger history are interrupted by Tom's voice. "*What* are you doing in there? What did I say about getting lost?"

"Too late, Tom," I mumble to myself.

I look over at the broken window frame I had squeezed through to see my husband's panicked face. I already know he's worried about setting out on his own in a domain full of dead people, so I hold my tongue and follow him.

I tuck the leather-bound diary under my shirt as I sneak a peek back over my shoulder at the empty mausoleum, knowing all too well that it is far from empty.

Shipwreck

Beneath the terrible weight
Coastal winds crash like claves
While in silence it waits.

Unseen to sails who pass too late
The feast from its corpse Sealife craves
Beneath the terrible weight

Alone below the rage and grate
Beyond cavernous, vaulted caves
In silence it waits.

A calm horror slumbers innate
And skeletal masts sway above staves
Beneath the terrible weight

…Five…Six…Seven…Eight…
It counts the crooked waves
While in silence it waits.

Even in its eroding state
The memory of former glory it saves
Beneath the terrible weight
While in silence it waits.

66

Burial at Sea

Wordless music
Hot tears on my tongue

A blurred black box
A slow-moving sun

Salty sea scents
The boat's bell has rung

Clay and ashes
All are here, but one

THE SIRENS OF WHITBY

1 April 1970

The salty scent of the sea filled my nose as I walked the narrow streets of the English seaside village of Whitby. Tiny bells rang as doors to sweet shops and vintage boutiques opened and shut, and the gray gulls that swooped over my head were about twice the size of the seabirds back in the States. All these curiosities lay in the shadow of the ancient ruins of Whitby Abbey, which towered over us atop the tallest cliff that loomed over the bay. I shivered and slid the zipper to my coat up to my chin.

I was one of twelve students on a study abroad trip for English Lit majors at my college. My professor was overly excited about this trip, since it was the setting that inspired Bram Stoker's *Dracula*, on which he had written his dissertation.

As I followed my class towards the ancient steps that led to the infamous graveyard of St. Mary's Church, the setting of

Stoker's novel itself, I noticed an old woman preparing a large fishing lure on one of the docks. The lure was unlike any I had ever seen. It was about three feet long and almost looked like a small human. I shuddered at the sight.

The woman's eyes met mine, but she said nothing. I glanced back at a couple girls from my class hurrying up the steps to the churchyard. I didn't want to fall too far behind, but my intrigue took over and I sauntered over to the dock where the woman and her strange contraption awaited.

The woman was dressed in a withered green raincoat, rubber boots, and suspenders; her wrinkled hands and face making her age seem almost undeterminable.

"That's a very strange fishing lure," I commented as she lugged the lure over her shoulder.

She grinned at me beneath her white bangs. "If truth be told, it's the fish that sometimes do the luring…" Her voice sounded slightly French, with a hint of a Cockney accent. She turned her back to me then and began shuffling down the dock to where a small fishing vessel was anchored.

Confused at her words, I followed. "What do you mean?"

She stopped and then turned to me, a thoughtful look in her eye. "You'd better return to your friends. No sense hanging around a crazy old fisherwoman."

"It's just my college class. We're visiting Whitby as part of a literature trip."

She shifted her gaze up towards the churchyard, its crumbling stones and haunting cemetery a lure of its own. "Well, lass, if you really are interested in stories, I have one you may not have heard before…"

15 August 1897

The day was the brightest I had witnessed over my two-week voyage, a good omen for sailors, our captain had said. I was seventeen and finally paying a visit to my cousin Wilhelmina in Whitby, who I hadn't seen in over a decade. Mama paid for my passage, and I was more than relieved to see a familiar face after almost a month at sea surrounded by a shipload of strangers.

Crowds of voyagers and unwashed sailors nudged me along as we marched off the boat, and my legs couldn't help but wobble atop the sturdy, unmoving ground.

Suddenly, I was almost toppled over by the mad rush of a violent hug as my cousin swung her arms around me. Shorter than I was, she was also much stockier, her arms nearly squeezing the air out of my lungs in greeting.

"Elizabeth!" She beamed, adjusting the pink shawl she wore around her shoulders. "How long has it been?"

"Too long, Cousin," I managed to squeak out before she finally released me. She weaved her arm through mine as I grabbed my bag, and we ambled away from the crowd of those disembarking.

"Just wait until you see Whitby!"

"It looks like a quaint place." My gaze shifted to the cobblestoned streets lined with stores and window-shoppers. No carriage was in sight, the streets far too narrow for such a bulky contraption, and a white lighthouse beamed at the crest of the horizon.

"Oh, that's only because the sun is out. When the fog rolls up from the ocean and the seagulls stop crying, that's when you must be on your guard." Her expression turned serious. "That's when the *Sirens* come out."

"The Sirens?" I repeated. "You honestly do not believe in those mythical creatures, do you?" Then I remembered who I was talking to. Wilhelmina had been obsessed with fairy tales ever since we were children, but I had hoped she had grown out of it by now. We were practically adults.

As if confirming my suspicions, she prattled on. "Have you read Mr. Stoker's new book *Dracula* yet? It was inspired by his trip to Whitby, you know. Oh, just wait until you see the churchyard! They say that is where the actual vampire is buried! And Mr. Stoker named his character Mina after me, you know!"

I raised an eyebrow. "But your name is Wilhelmina, *Wilhelmina*," I retorted, wondering if this entire trip would be filled with my cousin gushing about a new gothic romance novel.

She waved off my correction. "I've decided to shorten it. It sounds so much more romantic, don't you think? Anyway, we should give Mr. Stoker some credit for putting Whitby on the map. Local businesses here were faltering before he came, and now tourists cannot get enough of it!"

She babbled on like that for a while as we headed up the cobbled slope to the abbey. An old sailor barked at us as we began our ascent up the 199 steps. "Count your steps, or an omen will curse your next ones!"

"Are *all* sailors superstitious?" I found myself asking Wilhelmina—*Mina*—as I looked out at the harbor and rooftops sinking below us as we inched farther to the top of the cliff.

"When your life is in the hands of the sea, I've known many sailors to fear," she answered as we both arrived breathless at the top steps of the churchyard. Tombstones about as tall as my own petite frame loomed before us, some covered in blurred sandstone where thoughtful epitaphs were once engraved.

"How sad." I pointed to one teetering at the edge of the cliff that faced the ocean.

"They get that way from the salt of the sea." She shrugged, as if everyone was supposed to know that. As we traversed farther down the graveyard's path, Wilhelmina sputtered, "Come, I want to see where Dracula is supposed to be buried."

"How can the undead be buried?" a melodic voice said from behind me.

A young man and his companion bowed and approached us. The one who spoke had skin as fair as a baby's and his tousled hair was streaked with blond. His eyes were colored a striking blue that reminded me of sapphires. His companion was darker-haired with olive-toned skin and narrow eyes.

"Who are you?" my cousin blurted out, before I had a chance to address them. "I know everyone in Whitby, and I've never seen either of you before."

"We just came off the boat," he answered without hesitation, as if he was ready for the question.

My cousin turned to me, as if to confirm their story.

"Forgive me, but I just came off the boat, and I do not remember seeing either of you... I'm sure I would have remembered," I added with a slight blush. The dark-haired one smiled slightly. There were quite a few passengers on the ship, and I kept to myself for most of the voyage, so they may have been telling the truth. Regardless, why wouldn't they have been truthful?

Just then, a tall man dressed in a long flowing cape and a black top hat exited the church and headed over to where we all stood.

"I believe they are starting the tour," the blond-haired boy said as we all walked farther into the cemetery.

The tall man in black's voice quivered over the crowd. "…If you look closely, you can see the mists beginning to creep over the sea…the perfect setting for a vampire to hunt his prey…"

"What a load of codswallop," the dark-haired boy whispered as my cousin and her new beau listened eagerly to the tour guide. "What do you say we get out of here to somewhere less crowded?" Since I had been around nothing but crowds of people for the past month, the offer sounded tempting. But I barely knew this boy, and I couldn't leave my cousin.

I glanced at her, her own gaze fixed on the tour guide—a silly smile was plastered on her face, and her eyes gleamed at the tale about her new hero.

"Let us not go *too* far," I responded, and I followed him out of the cemetery. I knew my cousin or I should not have been without a chaperone, but how much danger could I be in with so many people around?

"Are you hungry?" he asked.

My stomach rumbled in answer. It had been a while since my last meal—if one could call a handful of ship's gruel an actual meal. I nodded, and he guided me over to one of the fish shops near the pier.

The sun no longer shined as brightly as it had when I first arrived, and a thick mist drew closer to the shoreline with every lap of the waves against the wooden pillars below our feet.

"So," he began, turning his gray eyes on me, "you are from France?"

I couldn't help but gasp slightly each time this young man spoke. His voice had a singsong quality to it, like his companion's, and I couldn't help but desire to hear more.

I nodded between mouthfuls of fresh cod. "Is my accent that noticeable?"

He shrugged and then winked at me. My heart fluttered at his striking gaze. I was never a girl people would describe as pretty; I was too tall for my age and hadn't developed yet in certain areas that dresses would complement. But this boy seemed to like me. And I liked that he liked me.

"Are you from Whitby, originally?" I asked, trying to flutter my eyelashes in a flirtatious manner.

His smile widened. I must have been doing it correctly. "Yes, but farther down the shoreline." He pointed down the pier. "Come, I'll show you."

He grabbed my hand. My heart leaped at his touch. I couldn't discern if it was solely because I was attracted to him or because his touch was coarse, like sand. We walked farther down the pier, and by the time we reached its end, the mist was so thick, I couldn't see much farther than a few feet down.

"Beyond." He pointed out into the mist.

I couldn't help but stifle a laugh. "Your eyesight must be better than mine. All I see is white mist from the sea."

He was no longer smiling. "Precisely."

The next thing I knew, I was falling…plunging…submerging into dark, icy water. I couldn't breathe. I opened my eyes to the murky undercurrent my body had just fallen into and saw traces of green—it must have been seaweed—and something else. A hand reaching for me across the murky green. I reached for it, knowing it to belong to the young man; he must have dived in after me. How gallant!

But as his hand gripped mine once more, I discovered that he was dragging me down farther into the gulf of dark water instead of upwards towards the air.

I tried to recoil my hand, but it was stuck in his sandpapered grasp. I used my other hand to pull his fingers from my skin, but his grip was strong. Doing the only other thing I could think of, I bit his hand as hard as I could.

It worked for a moment. He briefly loosened his grip and let out the strangest sound I had ever heard above or below the ocean's surface. It was a high-pitched screech, almost like a warning siren.

Down he dragged me until I became so weak from holding

my breath that I felt my head would explode. But then, right when I was about to give up, the monster's hold on me loosened. Squinting through the dark water, I could almost make out a set of pale hands grasping the creature's neck.

With one last ounce of adrenaline, I pushed against the salt, seaweed, and murky abyss, leaving my heavy skirt and petticoat behind, and I surfaced. The white mist blowing against my face was as arctic as the water. Which way was the shore? And where was my attacker? Where was my rescuer? Without pausing for further thought, I started swimming, hoping that I was heading in the right direction, until I saw a small light in the corner of my eye. The lighthouse!

I kicked as hard as I could towards the shimmering reflection of its light until I saw a familiar pile of wood marking the pier and heaved myself onto the rickety ladder at its end. I needed to get out of the water and away from this water demon. As much as it pained me to admit, I thought I would have rather faced off with a vampire. At least it would have been on land.

I shook the irrational thought from my fatigued mind and climbed up the rungs of the ladder until I reached the wooden surface of the pier. I trudged along the dock, shivering in my chemise and bloomers as I looked around for any sign of a living soul, but the wharf was abandoned. The fog must have scared the locals back into their homes, like Wilhelmina had said—and rightly so. Perhaps it *was* safer to be a little superstitious after all.

Wilhelmina. She could be in worse trouble than I was. What if the boy she was with was a monster too? I raced down the pier until I saw the infamous ruins of Whitby Abbey peeking through the mist. I scurried up all 199 steps—not bothering to count each one this time—until I reached St. Mary's Church cemetery, where the tour group used to be. All had dispersed except for the black-clad tour guide in his top hat. My attire (or lack of) must have been quite a shock to him, but this was a matter of life and death!

"Wh-where is my cousin and the boy she was with?" I managed to sputter out between my teeth chattering and gasps for air.

His mouth fell open at the sight of me and his eyes widened. "Madam, are you quite alright? You are soaked to the bone!" He took off his cloak and offered it to me to cover my indecency.

Not needing a reminder about my horrific ordeal, instead of accepting the cloak I found myself grabbing his lapels—a very unladylike thing to do—and repeating my question much louder.

"I-I don't know," he responded, a little frightened now. "I finished the tour, and everyone dispersed because of the fog. If you are referring to that know-it-all girl who kept asking where Dracula was buried, she and her blond companion headed down to the beach about ten minutes ago."

I careened out of his presence, down the unsteady terrain of the cliff to the beach below. My heeled boots sank into the sand as my feet pummeled the ground. Desperation rang in my throat as the beach absorbed each of my footsteps. "Wilhelmina! Mina! Where are you?"

Suddenly, right where the surf met the sand, I noticed an abandoned pink shawl. I took it in my hands, and my heartbeat began to speed up again as I realized where my cousin must have gone. Without even thinking, I trudged farther ahead into the crashing surf as it lapped against my already numb legs. Maybe she was still…

But before I could finish my wish, I was distracted by a tangle of light-colored seaweed floating towards me. Horror struck me as I realized that it was not seaweed, but hair.

Wilhelmina's hair.

I lunged for her and burst out into sobs as I flipped her over. Her pale cheeks and opened eyes, glazed over with death, would surely haunt my dreams. Wilhelmina lived in Whitby; she knew how to swim. Someone had drowned her. And I knew who.

I felt myself screaming as I scanned the beach for the blond-headed boy responsible for her demise but could see no one. He had gone back into the abyss from which he came.

20 August 1897

The funeral procession for Wilhelmina was like something out of a dream. The sun shone, the preacher said some things I could not discern through the shock emanating through my body and escaping through my tears. After much hesitation, I realized that

I should tell Wilhelmina's parents the truth about how she died. They were Whitby citizens after all. After witnessing the fear grasping the crowds enough to shut them up in their houses, I concluded that they may believe me. They did not.

It was easier for them to agree with the coroner who concluded that their daughter died of a drowning accident. I did not dare tell anyone else about what had really happened, and her parents forbade me from doing so. I knew they blamed me for her death, so the least I could do was obey their wishes.

After Wilhelmina's coffin was laid in the sea-swept earth of St. Mary's churchyard, I could not help but wonder how long the inscription on her own tombstone would last against the relentless salt-filled air. "Here lies Wilhelmina," her epitaph read. "At rest, but not forgotten."

She may have rested, but I knew that my own guilt could not. What if these monsters from the sea drowned another poor soul? How would I prevent it? How *could* I prevent it?

1 April 1970

"And rest in peace she did," the old woman continued. "That was, until her grave was found unearthed and cracked open two days later."

"What? How?" I'd remained silent until she relayed this sudden turn of events.

"The police didn't know what to make of her missing body, other than grave robbers. Was it my monster and his comrade? What more did they want with her? Hope seemed to escape all of us, until something curious washed up on shore a week later. Something with webbed fingers, sharp teeth, and blond hair. It looked like the boy who had been her companion, but different. Where his hands should have been, was a scaly green webbing of thick skin, and his teeth were sharper than I had remembered. No one could identify who this strange boy was, but they could gather where he had come from. Luckily it gave my own story I told Wilhelmina's parents some credence, but what puzzled the coroner most was the cause of death: drained of blood from two puncture-wounds in his neck…"

I couldn't stop my mouth from hanging open. Perhaps Bram Stoker gained more inspiration from Whitby concerning vampires than had been reported.

"Are you saying that Wilhelmina became a...*vampire?*"

The old woman did not bat an eyelash. "I am simply relating the evidence. But I couldn't help but wonder if the mysterious being who saved me from my own monster had anything to do with it."

I blinked. "How so? Did you ever find out who it was?"

"Or *what* it was."

I shuddered at her inference. Did she believe her attacker was taken down by a *vampire?*

"Do you think..." I paused before uttering, "*it* killed your attacker?"

"Alas, his body was never found."

"Is that why you are using that fishing lure?"

"Indeed, I will keep searching until he, too, no longer terrorizes Whitby."

Eager to get back to my class, and a little warier than before, I told her I had better be on my way.

"Be careful," she said as she again turned her back and headed towards the edge of the dock. "Sirens like to target foreigners."

With that warning in mind, I made my way off the pier and hurried up the sloping 199 steps to where my class was about to tour St. Mary's churchyard. A calm, eerie fog seemed to follow me, and a strong paranoia that vampires and Sirens would follow me in my wake began to settle in the pit of my stomach.

Upon arriving, I noticed the looming grave markers, some of their epitaphs far beyond recognition due to the spray from the sea. A black wooden sign greeted me on a post that looked like it had been erected in a more recent century. It read *Whitby Cathedral 1882* in gold paint, and underneath was a plain white paper taped onto the post that stated in black type: *Please do not ask us where Dracula's grave is located.*

I barely had time to smile when a voice came from behind me—a voice that sounded like waves crashing upon a shoreline. "How exactly does someone bury a vampire?"

Almost mechanically, I turned to the mysterious voice,

though I had an inkling about who it may have belonged to. "My thoughts exactly," I responded as I gazed upon the tan face, narrow eyes, and dark hair of a young man dressed in jeans and a Whitby t-shirt.

"You're American," he said. "Is this your first time in Whitby?"

I could barely hide the shiver creeping up from my paranoid stomach to my shoulders. This was all starting to sound very familiar. "Yeah, though I find large tour groups boring sometimes."

"Why don't we head farther down the pier, then, away from the madding crowd, so to speak?"

I gulped in answer. "Can we get something to eat first?" I asked, hoping to prolong the sinister design he had in mind.

"Indeed. I know just the place."

I'm sure you do. I followed him down the steps and to the corner fish shop that also served ice cream and *Welcome to Whitby* stickers. While he waited in line, I took my chance.

"I would like to take some pictures with my new camera," I remarked with a giggle and a smile, so he knew I was a girl interested in his mysterious attractiveness. He responded with one of his own smiles that both allured and frightened me, and I headed further down the pier.

When the fog was thick enough, I sprinted down the dock to where I had left the strange old woman. She had boarded her boat but had not yet set sail. I waved my arms at her, not wanting to shout and draw too much attention to myself. Luckily, she saw me. She turned off the engine and poked her head out the cabin window.

I approached the boat, out of breath. "I think," I began, taking in a few gulps of air, "I think I've found what you're looking for!"

The Obituary

Henry O'Donnell, 1972

His time had finally come
He renders as his face glares up from the page
Taunting his own suspicions
Of when his sand would run its course
He swallows his breakfast in silence
and ponders, can this truly be the end?
A life of light and shadow and then
A face upon a news-stained print?
Simple words upon parchment so thin?
He never had a chance to make his mark
…Will this be *his* end, too?
He crinkles the harbinger of bad news
And swallows his breakfast
In silence

82

Unmarked Graves

Iron latches congregate
around a dreary, lonely gate,
trapping our freedom from under.

Mortar seeps through our silent veins
holding dust from our bones in place
and vanquishes our surrender.

84

THE MOURNER

The funeral home was packed for a Saturday. Men adorned in black suits and women wearing black taffeta filled each chair and some even lined the back wall.

Apparently, the poor bloke in this coffin was of some importance.

I greeted everyone in my normal manner: a "Good afternoon, you have my deepest condolences," a firm shake of the hand, and a film of deep sympathy glossed over my eyes. After forty years in this profession, it had almost become my natural reaction to greeting anyone.

And then I saw her. Again.

Donning the same black gown that reached the floor, her shoulders draped in her signature woolen melancholy shawl, the woman sat, her eyes downcast under a hat draped in a short black veil.

I almost felt myself grumble at the sight of her. For the past three years, this woman had crashed almost every single funeral I had hosted in this parlor. At first I thought, *Maybe she is just acquainted with a lot of people*, but then her presence occurred more often than could be construed as mere popularity. Almost once a month she would sneak in and sit in the same folding chair by the door, dabbing at the dark rings under her eyes with a small white handkerchief. What was her purpose here? Did she sincerely mourn these people or was she simply morbid?

Maybe it was the scorching sun outside, or maybe it was the overcrowded number of guests clogging the entryway, but my temper was rather short that day.

She had overstayed her welcome.

I approached her trembling frame, and the frustration inside me subsided for a spell as I heard the muffled sobs emanate under her shallow breath.

I sighed, defeated. "Good afternoon," I mechanically remarked. "You have my deepest condolences."

She quieted her sobs long enough to whisper, "I know you have seen me here before, sir, and yet you have never stopped me from attending. Why?"

I shrugged, a little flustered at her directness. "Well, you don't seem to be bothering anyone." *Except for me*, I added in my head.

I sat down next to her as she resumed her quiet sobs. "I've heard of people like you, but I had never met any others."

She turned her veiled head to face me. Beneath the dark fabric I could just make out those familiar gray rings that lined the sockets of her eyes. How old *was* this woman?

"People like *me*?" she repeated, confused.

"You are a professional mourner, aren't you?" I asked, folding my arms in confident satisfaction that I had solved the mystery.

She sniffed in response and then lowered her head. "I do not cry out of sympathy, but out of guilt."

I was now intrigued. "Guilt? Might I suggest a church for that?"

She surprised me with a light laugh. "People like me wouldn't be welcome in a church."

I scoffed. "This isn't the dark ages; *everyone* is welcome at church!"

She returned the handkerchief to her nose, and I realized I may have overstepped my bounds. It was none of *my* business what happened in this woman's past; let her cry where she wanted to. I just couldn't help but feel sorry for the poor girl.

"It's a long story," she sniffed.

I relaxed into my chair. "I'm a good listener."

I didn't know what to expect from marriage. My parents seemed content enough in it, but was contentment all there was? It must have been. What else could there be? I had read about love in books and had seen glimpses of it here and there as I witnessed gentlemen holding the door for their wives and my father bringing fresh roses home for my mother. But how deep could it run? …Through to forever?

"You will make such a beautiful bride, my dear," my governess had told me as she stuck pins in the white lace that surrounded my body.

"Will I?" was all I managed to say. I had never met the man I was to marry, but I was scheduled to do so this evening with my parents. I didn't know much about him, except that he was about twice my age and owned a large textile mill. "It's for the good of the family," my parents had told me.

My fiancé's manor was dark and gloomy inside except for a few spare candles that lit our way to the dining hall. My husband-to-be—a chubby, muttonchop-bearded man of about forty-five years old—sat at the head of the narrow table, which had been chiseled in onyx, worn-out paint, darkly aged like him, as well as the rest of the house.

"It shall be a splendid church wedding!" my mother cooed as we were served the first course—a clear, watery broth that tasted faintly of duck.

My fiancé dropped his spoon into his bowl, which made a faint clink—an abrupt halt to whichever way the conversation was headed. "Oh no, that will not do."

My father dropped his spoon into his own bowl. "You do not expect my daughter to have a traditional Christian wedding? Whyever not?"

"It is the principle of the thing," he answered, causing confused gazes between my parents.

"The principle of what?" they asked in unison.

"I see we are at an impasse," he diverted. "May I suggest a lovely outdoor wedding in the church courtyard? I hear it is becoming all the rage in London."

My parents and I exchanged puzzled glances. But I knew my parents could not afford to let this advantageously wealthy bachelor escape from their grasps, so, much to their regret, they agreed to his terms.

"What will everyone think of an *outdoor* wedding? A wedding not in a church? I've never heard of such a thing. How very bizarre indeed…" My mother chattered on like a wind-up monkey toy for the rest of the night.

I did not know what to think. I had never heard of such a thing either, but my future was out of my hands.

The day approached with a dreary overcast and a knot in my stomach. Cousin Meredith had said weather like that was always a bad omen. I was not yet sure if I believed in such things, but after that day, anything was possible.

Our family and friends surrounded the tombstones of the churchyard, each one fearing raindrops with every roll of thunder that headed our way. At least my fiancé had agreed to have a priest marry us, as was my parents' condition.

The priest told us to join hands, and I could not help but feel an icy coldness instead of the warm skin I had expected to emanate from his hands.

"I know pronounce you man and…and…"

But before the priest could finish, his eyes widened in horror as he stared at the man holding my hands. For the person who held my hands was no longer a man, but a pale, red-eyed beast, teeth bared and salivating as he took a step closer to me, his grip now an icy vise.

Who was this devil? Without further warning, he sprung at me and tried to wrap his mouth around my neck, but I managed to recoil and yank my wrist away as screams erupted from the surrounding crowd. Other members of his "family" who shared his craving lunged at the closest members of my party.

I tried to run, but the train of my dress got caught under the heavy feet of my new husband who clawed his way through the cemetery grass over to where I lay frozen in fear.

Suddenly, the sharp blade of a large axe separated me from the menacing figure as it came down on one of his wrists. The creature squealed in pain and charged at the mysterious cloaked figure who held the axe poised over his shoulder, ready for another swing.

"Run!" the man who held the axe shouted to me. The word seemed to snap my senses back into focus and I followed the command, trying to dodge charging creatures as I did so.

I gathered what was left of my wedding gown train but did not get far before I tripped over something. Coming to, I realized it was a body. It was my father. His lifeless eyes stared past me, and I muffled a scream at the blood that seeped from the two gaping holes in the side of his neck.

Before I could stare any longer at this horrible scene, something cold and lifeless seized my wrist. It belonged to a being whose other hand was missing. My husband. Warm blood dripped from his mouth, which seemed to make his eyes redden deeper. I struggled against his unusually strong grip as he raised my hand to his nose and deeply inhaled the scent of my wrist. I had seen enough to know it was not the scent of my perfume he was savoring.

Just then, my other hand was grasped by another—one filled with the warm blood of life—and I tried to pull myself towards it, but I was still caught in the monster's grasp.

"She's mine!" my husband hissed at my rescuer, who, in answer, swung his axe just below the mutton chops lining my husband's cheekbones…slicing off his head.

I could almost hear the pounding of my heart as I witnessed

more bodies fall around me.

"There's too many!" the man with the axe shouted to me, and I let out another horrified shriek at the sight of my mother falling to the earth. He dragged my shocked body over the threshold of the church's entrance and slammed the heavy wooden door shut.

"Are you alright, Miss Price?" he asked me, setting his crimson-coated axe against a wooden pew.

I didn't know how to answer that. My family, my friends…were all dead.

After a moment, the only thing that could come out of my mouth was, "Of course not!"

I shrank into one of the wooden pews, trying to make sense of what I had seen, and then turned to face my rescuer. "Who are you, and how do you know my name?"

"I've been hunting your fiancé's vampire clan for weeks, but I'm afraid that we did not arrive in time… I am sorry for your loss."

I looked up at the young man. His dark hair framed his fair face and spots of blood clung to his stubbled cheeks. "*Vampire clan?*"

"I hunt monsters," he continued, as if reading the question on my face with his eyes. "In case you didn't already guess." He started picking up his axe and wiping the bloodstained blade with a kerchief he pulled from his pocket.

I must have sat there for ages. The reality of this strange story and even stranger truth I had just witnessed finally settling my understanding into the realm of a reality that I never knew existed. I stared up at him, a new resolve I hadn't expected bubbling from the fury I felt at the loss of my family. "Then I hunt them now too."

This was my first fight, and I was frightened but determined. Cemetery caretakers had noticed many graves unearthed and their corpses snatched in the past month, so we had no choice but to investigate.

I knew what Phillip was thinking. That I was an unprepared child. And in many ways, I was. But this cemetery was where my parents' bodies were buried, and I would not let another monster take them from me.

"Remember," Phillip coached, "ghouls eat the flesh of the dead. Do you remember how they come into being?"

I nodded, remembering my training. To procreate, ghouls feed their flesh to their victims. "If a human consumes the raw flesh of another ghoul, then they turn into a ghoul."

When we approached the graveyard, it was quiet, but I knew they were there. In the catacombs of the paupers or skulking behind the looming mausoleums of the rich, they were preparing for their nightly feast on the city's dead.

Phillip took my hand and led me through the wrought iron gate. I cringed at the slight squeak that escaped its hinges. And then I saw her. A young girl a few years younger than I, a bouquet of lilies in her arms, approached the freshly dug grave before her, not five headstones down from where we lingered.

"It's alright," I whispered to Phillip. "It is just a visitor."

"After dusk?" he asked me, raising an eyebrow.

He did make sense, but a little girl could not be such a hideous monster…could she?

I felt a leaf crunch beneath my boot, causing the little girl to turn and face me. Dark rings lined her pale skin. She looked sad, and something else… Hungry?

Suddenly, her demeanor changed, almost as quickly as my fiancé's had when he turned into his demonic, vampiric form just before his attack. Her eyes blackened and her face and limbs seemed to shrink into her bones, causing her to look as emaciated as a mummy. But she did not try to attack me. Instead, she grabbed something long and heavy leaning against the tombstone and pierced the earth with its spade. The deeper her blade struck the loose dirt, the more she snarled and salivated, yearning for the meal that awaited her. But before she could reach her desired goal, something swift and equally sharp soared at her head, and her body slumped to the ground. Dead.

I looked at my hand, which was poised in her direction. I had just thrown the knife I had concealed in my boot for this moment. Phillip had told me that stabbing a ghoul in the brain was the surest way to defeat them. I grimaced at what I had just done, a feeling of disgust and shock rising in my throat.

Before I could pause for further thought, something growled behind us. We turned to face two ghouls who were older than the young girl. I wondered if they had been her parents, and then a bubbling regret arose inside me as my own parents' faces came to the forefront of my mind.

My hesitation would be my downfall.

Phillip managed to pin one of them down to the ground, but he was soon overcome. Before I could help him, the woman had grabbed me by the ankles and was attempting to claw up my torso. She soon pinned my arms over my head and was poised to take a bite out of my face, her teeth being her only weapon. My neck was the only thing I could move so, without even thinking, I lunged at her and took a large bite out of her cheek. She let out a distraught shriek as black blood oozed from her face, and she scurried away from me.

I spit out the revolting taste of death from my mouth, but I knew it was too late. I had tasted the dead. And now, nothing could stop me from becoming one of them. Just as Phillip had warned me.

Phillip!

I struggled to find my bearings as blackness seeped into my vision. The transformation had begun. I reached for where I thought Phillip had fallen, but I felt cold skin instead. The skin of the ghoul he had killed. And then I sensed another body. I inched closer to the body next to the ghoul and screamed when I felt the lifeless face. Phillip's face.

The darkness had then all but consumed my sight and mind. I had to now live the life of that which I had sought to destroy.

The atmosphere in the funeral parlor was as cold and somber as this woman's story had been.

"So, each funeral I've seen you attend, you have…" I gulped

at the words, "*consumed* the body who it is for?"

The woman in black dabbed at her sunken eyes once more. "I do not mourn that they have departed, but what they have left behind…and what I must do to them to survive. And I *will* survive until I have rid the world of all monsters."

I was both curious and scared now, wondering if she would make a meal of *me*. But I had a feeling if she wanted to kill me, she would have already done so. "How long have you been searching for them?"

For the first time since I had seen her today, the mourner shifted her gaze to the coffin at the end of the hall. "Too long. And yet, not long enough."

94

THE HOUSE OF ONE HUNDRED FACES

13 Ways of Looking at a Funeral

I.

Wordless music casts
Hot tears on his tongue
At the sight of a blurred black box

II.

A slow-moving sun heralds
Salty sea scents while
A copper bell clangs

III.

The chill of winter brings
All of them here—
Except for one

IV.

Clay and ashes beneath green grass
Reveal a watchman; was he standing at
that headstone before?

V.

The sharp shots fire while
Witnesses feel the shrapnel
Echo through their own bones

VI.

The shell is empty,
But she's still felt among
The guests. Alive and well.

VII.

Gray, black, and white feathers shroud the
Long-necked onlookers who search the
frozen ground for breakfast

VIII.

They weep—
All except for her—
Dry cheeks instead border a grin

IX.

Little feet chase the box that holds
Her Mamma as it lowers to the earth;
Why does she leave her here alone?

X.

He raises his hand
To solute his stiff comrade…
But only one finger makes it

XI.

Garbed in plaid
The bagpiper plays
On and on and on

XII.

An amber-tipped arrow
Salutes the distant grave
Before setting its mark ablaze

XIII.

Alone he watches the crowd with a smile—
He had expected less—
He tiptoes away, remaining invisible

The Dark

Granting sway to malice
Not knowing what it hides
A violent past it attracts
Those with wicked sides

But do not fear
The light is near
One more night till dawn

While it preys upon your dreams
It's fading fast…soon gone

Stalking empty streets
And the corner in your room
It lies in wait to frighten,
This harbinger of doom

While monsters creep
You seek to sleep
And tell the truth from lies

The only place it now afflicts
Are realms behind your eyes

ABOUT THE AUTHOR

W. M. Ashley (an author pseudonym of Ashley Weaver) is a native of the Pacific Northwest who likes to read and write "wholesome horror" and historical fiction. When she isn't teaching college writing courses, penning children's books under the pen name Imogene Plum, or playing with her mini goldendoodle, Molly, she's probably on a history hunt, meandering through a cemetery, or watching mudlarking videos on YouTube. Follow her writing projects at wmashleyauthor.com and Instagram: @wmashleyauthor.

DID YOU LIKE THIS ANTHOLOGY?

If you would like more spooky content, then check out:

The House of One Hundred Faces
Anthology Coloring Book,
coming September 2025!

This visual showcase of the anthology contains a collaboration of coloring pages from various indie illustrators.

Check out this creative addition to the anthology and let your imagination soar!